WELCOME TO RAVENS PASS

THE SLEEPER

by Steve Brezenoff
illustrated by Tom Percival

W9-BOO-073

Ravens Pass is published by Stone Arch Books
a Capstone imprint
1710 Roe Crest Drive
North Mankato, Minnesota 56003
www.capstonepub.com

Copyright © 2013 by Stone Arch Books. All rights reserved. No part of this publication may be reproduced in whole or in part, or stored in a retrieval system, or transmitted in any form or by any means, electronic, mechanical, photocopying, recording, or otherwise, without written permission of the publisher.

Library of Congress Cataloging-in-Publication Data
Brezenoff, Steven.
The sleeper / written by Steve Brezenoff ; illustrated by Tom Percival.
     p. cm. -- (Ravens Pass)
  Summary: The Galactic Expansion Home for Lost Children, otherwise known in Ravens Pass as the Old Orphanage, is actually full of alien children ready to take over the planet--but at least one of them may actually be a human spy.
  ISBN 978-1-4342-3792-7 (library binding) -- ISBN 978-1-4342-4211-2 (pbk.) -- ISBN 978-1-4342-4654-7 (ebook)
  1. Extraterrestrial beings--Juvenile fiction. 2. Orphanages--Juvenile fiction. 3. Horror tales. [1. Extraterrestrial beings--Fiction. 2. Orphanages--Fiction. 3. Horror stories.] I. Percival, Tom, 1977- ill. II. Title.

  PZ7.B7576Sl 2012
  813.6--dc23
                                   2012003961

Graphic Designer: Hilary Wacholz
Art Director: Kay Fraser

Photo credits:
iStockphoto: chromatika (sign, backcover); spxChrome (torn paper, pp. 7, 13, 19, 27, 37, 45, 51, 63, 67, 73, 79, 83) Shutterstock: Milos Luzanin (newspaper, pp. 92, 93, 94, 95, 96); Robyn Mackenzie (torn ad, pp. 1, 2, 96); Tischenko Irina (sign, pp. 1, 2); Photographic textures and elements from cgtextures, composited by Tom Percival: (Front cover and pp. 10, 15, 25, 30, 39, 46, 59, 64, 69, 75, 81, 87, 93)

Printed in the United States of America.
122016   010205R

Between where you live and where you've been, there is a town. It lies along the highway, and off the beaten path. It's in the middle of a forest, and in the middle of a desert. It's on the shore of a lake, and along a raging river. It's surrounded by mountains, and on the edge of a deadly cliff. If you're looking for it, you'll never find it, but if you're lost, it'll appear on your path.

The town is **RAVENS PASS**, and you might never leave.

TABLE OF CONTENTS

Chapter 1

THE OLD ORPHANAGE

Most residents of Ravens Pass thought of the graveyard as the end of town. After all, there was no reason to go past.

All the shops and restaurants were on Main Street. The only factory in town was on Industrial Boulevard, near the highway.

The schools and the library were just a block off Main, close to the park. And every house was on one of the side streets.

Well, every house except one: the Galactic Expansion Home for Lost Children. Or, as everyone in Ravens Pass called it, the Old Orphanage.

It was a five-story, rickety old house. On gray, cold days, if you were brave enough to take a walk past the cemetery, you'd see kids from ages two to twenty playing on the big overgrown front yard. And sitting on the porch, in their old rocking chairs, would be the two men who had been running the Old Orphanage since it was founded.

No one in Ravens Pass knew their names, of course, but they would all know the men on sight. Mr. Jinks was the short one. He wore colorful, outlandish suits: his jackets all had tails, his collars all had ruffles, and his pants all had patterns or stripes or plaids. He usually carried a cane, too, and he never smiled.

Mr. Flute was the tall one, nearly seven feet tall. He wore black wool pants and a black wool sweater. When the two men were in town — to pick up groceries or diapers — Mr. Flute always had a "hello" and a smile for everyone.

But usually the residents of Ravens Pass only saw the men's car: a long black station wagon with tinted windows.

Every so often the long black car would move slowly through town. It would puff a cloud of smoke behind it. Its engine would blast and boom. Then the car would head onto the highway and vanish.

It always came back, though, of course. Whether it was gone for a few days or a few months, when the car came back, a few new children would appear at the Old Orphanage.

No one knew where the two men found their children, and no one asked.

They should have, though, because Mr. Jinks and Mr. Flute were not ordinary men, and these were not ordinary children.

They were aliens, and they were planning to destroy Earth.

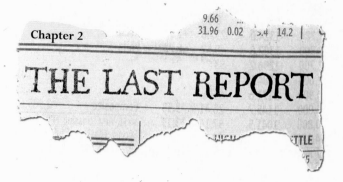

Chapter 2

THE LAST REPORT

Three boys walked along Main Street. It was a gray afternoon, and most Ravens Pass kids were in school. But these three kids were from the Old Orphanage, and they weren't enrolled in the public school.

"I hate this stupid town," said Tomm, the dark-haired boy. He kicked a stone and it bounced into the street.

"Me too," said his friend and fellow orphan Garrison. Garrison was tall and lanky with reddish floppy hair.

The third boy, Herk, sighed and coughed. His belly shook. "It won't be around much longer," he said.

Tomm nodded. Like the other kids in the orphanage, he felt bad that ships from the home world would soon arrive to destroy Earth. Earth was a pretty nice place, and he'd had a good time there.

But Mr. Jinks and Mr. Flute reminded them again and again that they need the minerals at the Earth's center to power their home world. They didn't have a choice.

"I handed in my last report this morning," Herk said. "It was a geological study."

Garrison chuckled. "What else?" he said. "All I've done since I got to this planet is geological studies."

Tomm shrugged. "Me too," he said. "And my last report is due this afternoon. In fact, I should probably head back to the house. Mr. Jinks hates when my reports are late."

"And they usually are," Herk said. He elbowed Tomm in the ribs and laughed.

The boys reached the pizza parlor and Garrison stopped. "Let's eat first," he said.

"I don't think I have time," Tomm said.

"Listen," Garrison said. "If all our final reports are due, you know what that means."

Herk's eyes went wide. He nodded. "It means the attack will begin soon," he said.

"Exactly," Garrison said. "So this might be our last chance for some pizza."

Tomm thought it over.

Without any Earthlings around, there might never be pizza again. "Okay," he said. "But let's get the pizza to go."

Chapter 3

A MEETING

Aug. 3

The boys had to run to make it back to the house in time. Mr. Jinks and Mr. Flute were both standing on the porch when they got there.

"Hello, sirs," Tomm said. "Sorry we were almost late." He dropped his backpack at their feet as Garrison and Herk slipped past the men and into the orphanage.

"Hello, Tomm," Mr. Flute said. He smiled. Mr. Jinks didn't say anything, and he didn't smile. He just stared at Tomm, waiting.

Tomm dropped to one knee and unzipped his bag. "I have my final report right here," he said. He found the thick, bound report and pulled it out. Then he handed it to Mr. Flute.

"Thank you, Tomm," Mr. Flute said, grinning.

"So," Tomm said. "If that's the final report, I guess the mission is about to really get started, huh?"

Mr. Flute, still smiling, looked at Mr. Jinks. Mr. Jinks looked back, closed his eyes briefly, and shook his head.

"Well," Mr. Flute said to Tomm, "we will see. First, join Mr. Jinks and me in the meeting room with the rest of the children. We have something very important to discuss."

Tomm was surprised. They usually had meetings only when a new "orphan" arrived.

But Mr. Jinks and Mr. Flute hadn't left the Old Orphanage in weeks. There were no new orphans.

The two men turned and went inside the house. Tomm hurried to zip up his backpack. Then he ran through the front door and started down the hall toward the meeting room.

When he remembered that he'd left the front door open, he quickly ran back to close it.

When Tomm finally got to the meeting room and found a seat, he was out of breath. He was also the last orphan to get to the meeting.

Mr. Flute smiled at him when he sat down. Mr. Jinks did not.

"Hello," Mr. Flute said to the gathered orphans. "As some of you have guessed, our mission is about to move into its final stage."

The orphans smiled and whispered to each other, things like, "Finally," "Here we go," and "It's gonna be so cool!"

But then Mr. Jinks cleared his throat. The room hushed. Everyone sat bolt upright in their chairs. Mr. Jinks never spoke, and he almost never made a sound.

Mr. Jinks coughed. A girl in the back — one of the newest orphans — burst into tears as soon as she heard the sound.

"Now, now," Mr. Flute said, smiling. He put up his hands to calm the orphans. "Mr. Jinks, let's not get too angry. This will all be settled."

Mr. Jinks crossed his arms. He stared at the far wall.

"Thank you," Mr. Flute said.

He turned back to the orphans. He sighed, still smiling, and pulled a chair from the corner. He sat down and leaned toward the children.

"Orphans," he said, "I'm afraid this is a serious matter." He sounded sad and worried. Still, his smile was big and bright.

He showed all his teeth when he smiled. Tomm thought it made Mr. Flute seem a little scary sometimes — like when something serious was going on.

"As you know, a fleet of ships from the home world is due to arrive very soon," Mr. Flute went on. "However, the ships are waiting, just outside the Solar System, because their sensors have discovered something . . . disturbing."

Mr. Jinks coughed again. Several orphans flinched in their chairs.

"During one of their routine scans," Mr. Flute said, "the ships detected an Earthling."

The orphans leaned forward. They looked at one another. *So what?* Tomm thought. *Obviously Earth is covered with Earthlings!*

Mr. Jinks sniffled and sneezed.

"The Earthling is living here," Mr. Flute said, "in the Orphanage."

Mr. Jinks stamped his brightly colored boots on the meeting room floor. He balled up his fists. He coughed and gritted his teeth.

"We have a spy," Mr. Flute said. "A spy living among us."

A little boy screamed.

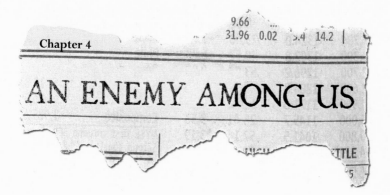

Chapter 4

AN ENEMY AMONG US

The orphans gasped and whispered nervously to each other.

"Who is it?" Herk shouted.

Mr. Flute shook his head. "We don't know," he said.

"Can't we find out?" Garrison said.

"We are waiting for equipment right now," Mr. Flute said. "When it arrives, we will scan everyone at the orphanage. Then we'll know."

"When will it arrive?" asked one of the older girls.

"Tomorrow morning," Mr. Flute said.

"By then the spy might escape," Herk said, "or kill us all!"

Mr. Flute laughed. "Try not to worry," he said. "Why, if the spy wanted to kill us, he or she would have already."

Mr. Jinks sneezed. He was so angry that Mr. Flute jumped up from his chair and escorted him to their private study.

The orphans waited until the meeting room door closed. Then they burst into excited chatter.

"How can this be?" Herk whispered. He and Garrison stood next to Tomm's chair. "How could someone here be a spy?"

Tomm could only shrug.

The whole thing was really weird. How could any of the orphans be an Earthling spy? He'd known most of them his whole life. Mr. Flute and Mr. Jinks had brought him, Garrison, and Herk to the orphanage more than ten years ago, when they were just babies.

Garrison peered around the room. "I wonder who it is," he said quietly.

Tomm stood up. He nodded toward the door. "Come on," he whispered.

Herk and Garrison nodded back. The three boys quietly left the meeting room. Then they ran through the orphanage's back door.

At the shed, they each grabbed a BMX bike. Then they took off.

"We have to figure this out," Tomm said as the three boys sped through the winding walkways of the cemetery on their bikes.

Herk pedaled hard around a tight bend. Then he hopped his BMX over a pothole and landed in the grass. He skidded to a stop. Garrison and Tomm stopped too.

"Who do you think it could be?" Herk asked.

Tomm shook his head. "It must be one of the new kids," he said. "I mean, we would have noticed something over the years if one of the orphans had been an Earthling, right?"

Garrison nodded. "Earthlings smell different, for one thing," he said.

Herk laughed. "And they don't know a thing about geology," he added.

Tomm nibbled on his fingernails. He thought about all the orphans who had arrived in the last year or so.

Garrison must have been thinking about the same thing, because he snapped his fingers. "Mabel," he said. "She just got here three weeks ago."

Herk got off his bike and sat down. "Could be her," he said. "I wouldn't be surprised. We sure don't know her very well."

"I don't know," Tomm said. "She's only six months old. She wouldn't be much good as a spy."

"Good point," Garrison admitted. "Maybe it's the boy Mr. Flute brought here last June."

"You mean Carl?" Tomm asked. "The one who never talks to anyone?"

"That's the guy," Garrison said. "He's always listening to his headphones. Maybe that's how he communicates with his Earthling bosses."

Herk shook his head. "Nope," he said. "Carl is clean. I've seen him eat."

"Oh, right," Herk said. "Earthlings eat with their mouths."

Tomm and Garrison shivered. "Gross,"Tomm said.

Something snapped nearby. It sounded like a branch.

Herk jumped to his feet. "Did you guys hear that?" he asked.

Tomm and Garrison nodded.

"Someone's watching us,"Tomm whispered. "Eavesdropping."

Garrison put his finger to his mouth. Then he tiptoed past Herk, toward the bushes along the graveyard's fence.

Something rustled in the bushes.

"He's in there!" Garrison shouted. Herk and Tomm ran toward the bushes just as a figure came speeding out and ran deep into the cemetery.

"It must be the spy!" Tomm said. "After him!"

Chapter 5

THE ACCUSED

The three boys took off running, dodging gravestones and tree trunks and low-hanging branches.

"Did you get a look at him?" Herk asked, gasping for breath as he ran.

Garrison shook his head.

"He was moving too fast," Tomm said. He spotted someone running behind a small stone building near the north gate. "There!" he shouted.

"Go around the other side," Herk said. "We'll surround him."

The boys split up and blocked off the building's corners. Tomm headed right for the north gate.

"Aha!" Tomm said. "You're trapped!"

"Don't hurt me!" the boy said.

Tomm, Herk, and Garrison stood around the younger boy.

"It's just Little Nelson," Herk said with a chuckle.

"So what are you sneaking around for?" Garrison asked.

Nelson twisted up his face and looked at the older boys. "What are you three doing in the cemetery?" he asked in a squeaky voice. "Having a secret meeting?"

"What?" Tomm said. He elbowed Herk lightly. "He thinks we're spies!"

"Are you?" Nelson asked.

"There's only one spy," Herk pointed out. "Mr. Flute said so."

"No he didn't," Nelson said. "Not really."

"Anyway, we've been in the orphanage for more than ten years," Tomm said. "Say, when did you come to the orphanage, anyway?"

Nelson shrugged.

"I know," Garrison said. "He's only been here for eight months. Right, Nelson?"

Nelson shrugged again. "I guess," he admitted.

Herk leaned back on his heels. Then he took a couple of steps back. "It seems to me that if any of us is the spy, it's probably Nelson here," he said.

"No way!" Nelson said.

The older boys circled around Nelson. "We should bring him to Mr. Jinks," Herk said.

Garrison snarled. "We should bring him directly to the high command," he said.

Tomm shook his head. "That's too good for him," he said. "We should take care of him right here in the graveyard."

"Ahh!" Nelson yelled. He tried to run, but Herk grabbed him. "Let me go!" Nelson cried.

Then Tomm, Herk, and Garrison started laughing. "Don't worry, Nelson," Tomm said. "We know it's not you."

"Yeah," Herk said. He patted the younger boy on the back. "You got that cut on your finger in the kitchen last night, remember? We all saw your blood."

"Oh yeah," Nelson said quietly. The four boys stood there quietly a minute.

"Hey, I saw a movie once," Nelson said. "It was about a spy who didn't even know he was a spy."

"What?" Tomm asked, frowning.

Nelson nodded. He bent down and picked up a little rock. "Yup," he said. "See, he was a good guy, but when the bad guys called him on the phone and said the right word, he would suddenly become a bad guy."

"What's your point?" Garrison said.

"They called him a sleeper," Nelson said. "So the spy could be me, or one of you, and we wouldn't even know!"

"That is the stupidest thing I've ever heard," Herk said.

"Yeah," Tomm said. "You watch too many of those dumb Earth movies."

"We better get back," Garrison said, "or the rest of the orphans will think *we're* the spies."

Nelson jogged off toward the gate. The three older boys found their bikes and started for home.

"Hey," Garrison said. He pedaled harder until he was in front of the other two. "Let's race back."

Garrison sped along the cemetery path toward the exit. "I'll beat you both!" Tomm shouted gleefully as he skidded into the street.

"Look out!" Herk called. But it was too late.

Tomm was moving too fast, and so was the little black sports car that zoomed past the cemetery. It slammed into Tomm's bike and sent him flying onto the sidewalk.

Chapter 6

BIG TROUBLE

"Tomm!" Herk shouted. He jumped off his bike and ran to his friend. Garrison was close behind.

Meanwhile, the little black sports car stopped. One of the tinted windows rolled down slightly.

"Hey," Garrison yelled at the driver. "You hit our friend!" The window slid back up, and the car sped off.

"Come back here!" Herk shouted. But the car didn't stop. Soon it was around the corner and out of sight.

"Are you okay?" Garrison asked.

Tomm rolled around on the sidewalk and groaned in pain.

"I don't see any blood," Herk said.

Garrison looked around. Somehow, a few residents of Ravens Pass — the Earthling residents — had heard the crash. They were coming, running toward the boys.

"Good," Garrison said, "because if these people saw Tomm's blood, they'd probably call the Army."

The Earthlings gathered around. One woman pulled out her phone. "I'll call for an ambulance," she said.

"No!" Herk said. He jumped to his feet. "We'll get Mr. Jinks and Mr. Flute from the orphanage. They'll want to take care of Tomm themselves."

The woman made a confused face and dialed 911. "I don't know," she said. "I couldn't live with myself if I didn't try to help." Then she said into the phone, "A boy has been hit by a car. Please send an ambulance right away."

Garrison and Herk looked at each other. They both knew an ambulance would mean trouble. All the orphans had been told over and over not to end up at a doctor's office or a hospital. Their true identities as aliens would be easily discovered.

"We better get help," Herk whispered to Garrison.

Garrison nodded, and the two boys jumped onto their bikes and sped off.

"Where are they going?" the woman with the phone asked.

The other Earthlings shrugged.

A siren wailed not far off. "Well, here comes help, at least," the woman said. And soon Tomm was being loaded into the back of the ambulance. He felt two people lift him up. Then he felt the emergency van speeding through Ravens Pass toward the hospital.

He couldn't think straight. But he had the sense that he was in big, big trouble. Then he passed out.

Chapter 7

A MEMORY

Aug. 3

"Ugh," Tomm said. He woke up bleary-eyed and confused. He was in a white room. A big window on his left showed a gray and dreary sky over an empty parking lot.

Tomm rolled his head. On his right was a machine on wheels. Wires and tubes came out of it. He traced them with his eyes to find they were plugged into his arm. One of them led to a tube up his nose. Past the machine was another big window, but this one faced the hallway.

Men and women in white coats and blue pants walked by. They all seemed to be in a big hurry.

I'm at the hospital, Tomm realized. *There are doctors everywhere. They'll find out I'm an alien.*

He tried to move, but his hands and waist were buckled to the bed. He couldn't budge.

"Oh no," Tomm muttered. *They already know. They know what I am. They've tied me to the bed so I can't escape.*

Tomm lay there and closed his eyes.

He remembered all the warnings Mr. Flute had given him and his friends at the Old Orphanage.

* * *

One hot afternoon when they were little, Tomm, Garrison, and Herk were running through the sprinkler in the backyard. They laughed and jumped and played in the cool spray of water.

It was one of Tomm's earliest memories.

Mr. Jinks and Mr. Flute sat on the back porch, watching them. Mr. Flute smiled and shouted things like, "Great jump," and "That looks fun, doesn't it, Mr. Jinks?"

Mr. Jinks just nodded and rocked in his chair.

Then Garrison tripped. His foot caught on the sprinkler and he sprawled across the lawn. His knee struck a rock.

"Ow!" he cried out. "Owie!"

Mr. Flute and Mr. Jinks jumped from their chairs. Herk and Tomm just stood there, watching.

Tomm remembered sucking his thumb as he watched his friend roll around on the grass in pain.

Mr. Jinks scooped Garrison up from the grass and held him in his arms like a baby. Mr. Flute stood close by and peered at Garrison's knee.

The cut was deep. Garrison's yellow blood streamed out and ran down his leg.

"Hurts!" Garrison said through his tears.

Mr. Flute smiled, as usual, and pressed his black handkerchief against the cut. "There," he said. "You will be all better soon." He turned to Herk. "Run inside to the bathroom and get a bandage," he said. "Do you know where they are?" Herk nodded excitedly. Then he ran inside.

"You'll be fine in no time," Mr. Flute said. Then he laughed and added, "Did you know that Earthlings have red blood?"

Garrison stopped crying and looked at Mr. Flute's smiling face. "Isn't that funny?" Mr. Flute asked kindly.

Garrison nodded. Tomm thought, *Red blood? Gross.*

Herk arrived and held out a bandage. "Here, sir," Herk said.

Mr. Flute took the bandage and put it on Garrison's cut. By then the bleeding had all but stopped. Mr. Jinks put Garrison gingerly back on his feet.

Tomm hurried over and gave Garrison a hug. The three boys stood together at Mr. Jinks's and Mr. Flute's feet.

"Boys," Mr. Flute said, "we're very different from the other people in Ravens Pass. Did you know that?"

The three boys nodded.

"In fact," Mr. Flute said as he put his arms around the boys and led them inside, "if an Earthling had been here and seen Garrison fall, we would be in big, big trouble."

"How come?" Tomm asked. He looked up at Mr. Flute eagerly.

"Come with me," Mr. Flute said. "I'll try to explain."

Mr. Flute led the boys into the kitchen. Mr. Jinks followed and went to the freezer. He pulled out three ice pops. The boys ran to Mr. Jinks and each grabbed a pop.

"Because," Mr. Flute said as he sat down at the kitchen table, "they would have seen his yellow blood."

"So?" Herk said. He sloppily devoured his blue ice pop.

"Earthling blood is red," Mr. Flute said, grinning. "Before long, a team of Earth scientists would take Garrison from us and start doing experiments on him."

"Spearmints?" Tomm stuttered.

"Experiments," Mr. Flute corrected. He took a deep breath. "If something like this happened to you, Tomm, they might even cut you open."

Garrison cringed. Herk struggled to swallow a big chunk of his ice pop.

Tomm's eyes went wide and he sniffled. "Cut me open?" he repeated. His eyes filled with huge tears.

Mr. Jinks coughed.

"We're upsetting Mr. Jinks," Mr. Flute said. He stood up. "The point is, boys, whenever you are in trouble — any kind of trouble at all — you come right to us, okay?"

He leaned down and put a hand on Tomm's shoulder. "If you're ever hurt, you come right to Mr. Jinks and me," Mr. Flute repeated.

Tomm nodded. "Okay," he said.

"You have to promise," Mr. Flute said. He looked at Garrison and Herk, too. "The three of you. You each must promise."

So they promised.

* * *

Tomm opened his eyes. He had fallen asleep, but he was still in that hospital bed, and he was still tied down.

Standing over him now, though, were two Earthling doctors.

"He's waking up," one of them said.

They leaned over Tomm and looked him in the face. Both men tried to smile, but Tomm could tell they were upset.

"We've called the Old Orphanage," one of them said.

"That's where you live, isn't it?" the other asked.

Tomm nodded.

"Good," said the first doctor. Then he held up a file—Tomm's patient file.

"We took your X-rays while you were unconscious," said the second doctor.

"And we found something," said the first doctor. "Something very . . . alarming."

Chapter 8

A COVER-UP

They know! Tomm thought. He struggled against the buckles and straps that held him in the bed.

"Please," the doctor said. "Don't try to move. You'll only make things worse."

"You already have three broken bones," said the other doctor. "Please try to be still." He held up a huge needle. "Or else," he said, "we'll have to sedate you." Tomm stopped wriggling.

"That's better," said the first doctor. Then he slipped the X-ray onto a darkened screen.

He was about to click the screen on when his beeper went off. The other doctor's did too. They both looked at their beepers. "We have to go," one of them said. "We'll be back as soon as we can. Try not to struggle."

Tomm watched them leave. He saw them rush past the window and disappear down the hall.

After they'd been gone for a couple of minutes, Tomm started wriggling again, trying to get out of the straps. It hurt his arm badly, but he had no choice. If he couldn't get out, they'd cut him open — experiment on him! It took all his strength, weak as he was, but he managed to free his left arm.

His hand was numb, but he tried desperately to unbuckle the strap across his waist. It wouldn't open.

Chapter 9

ESCAPE

Aug. 3

Tomm let his head fall back onto the pillow. He caught his breath and stared at the ceiling.

He listened to the voices in the hallway and the pinging and beeping of machines. He heard phones ringing and footsteps moving quickly down the halls. He heard the elevator ding.

Phones! Tomm realized.

He looked to his left. On the little table next to the bed was a phone.

Getting his hand on the phone hurt even more than struggling against the straps had hurt. But he managed.

He held the big heavy mouthpiece between his ear and his shoulder. With his free hand, he reached over and dialed. It took a long time, since he couldn't quite see the numbers and had to do it by feel. Finally, the phone rang on the other end.

"Hello?" said a breathless young voice.

Tomm could hear other voices, some of them loud and upset, in the background.

"Herk?" Tomm said. "Is that you?"

"Tomm!" Herk said. "Boy, am I glad to hear from you."

"Why are you answering the phone?" Tomm asked. "What's going on down there? Where's Mr. Flute?"

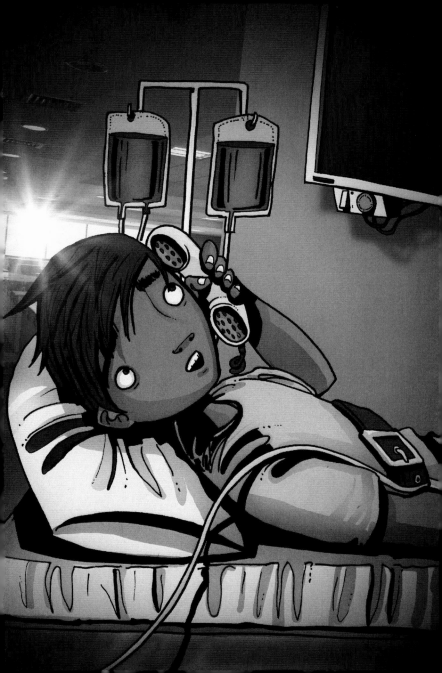

"He and Mr. Jinks are on their way to see you right now," Herk said.

Then Herk's voice changed. He was practically whispering. "Listen, Tomm," he said. "Something has happened. You have to get out of there."

"I know," Tomm said. "I'm trying to escape, but I could only get my arm free. That's why I called."

"No, you don't understand," Herk said. "Mr. Flute and Mr. Jinks are coming to get you."

Tomm heard voices in the hallway.

"Wait a second, Herk," Tomm said. He leaned up to look out the window to the hallway. The doctors were walking back.

"I have to go," Tomm snapped into the phone. Then he hung up quickly and put his left arm at his side.

"Sorry about that," one of the doctors said as they came in. They both stood near the X-ray screen.

One of them clicked it on. "Now then," he said. He pointed at the X-ray. It was of a human leg. Parts of the leg bone had big cracks.

"This bone is broken here," the doctor said, "and here."

There was a light tap on the window to the hallway. Tomm looked and saw Mr. Jinks and Mr. Flute waving at him.

The doctor opened the door and the two orphanage directors came in.

"Hello, Tomm," Mr. Flute said. "Are they treating you well down here?" He winked.

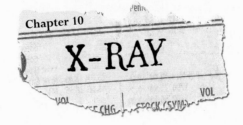

X-RAY

Tomm was thrilled to see his two guardians. He wanted to sit up and cheer. The straps wouldn't let him sit up, though.

"What are these restraints for?" Mr. Flute asked, running to the bedside.

The doctors glanced at each other. "Those are for his protection," one of them said.

"You've arrived just in time," the other doctor said. He walked over to the lighted X-ray display.

"As we were telling Tomm here," the doctor went on, "the X-rays are quite alarming."

Mr. Flute and Mr. Jinks looked pointedly at Tomm. His eyes went wide. This was it: the doctors were about to show their hands. It was over.

The orphanage, the orphans, Mr. Flute and Mr. Jinks — the entire mission was about to come to a crashing halt.

The doctor pulled out the X-ray of Tomm's leg and slipped in another one. This one was of Tomm's chest.

Tomm stared at it. Surely this X-ray would give him away as an alien. The differences between Earthlings and aliens didn't stop at the color of their blood.

Outside, aliens and Earthlings looked the same. But inside, everything was different, and Tomm's X-ray wouldn't look anything like a normal Earthling X-ray.

As the doctor moved out of the way, Tomm's breath caught in his throat. This X-ray showed one heart, one stomach, and two lungs. It couldn't be his X-ray.

The doctors pointed at the image. They said something about broken ribs.

But Tomm barely heard them. He stared at Mr. Flute and Mr. Jinks. Mr. Jinks coughed. Mr. Flute winked and smiled.

Relief flooded Tomm. He rested his head and watched the doctors. His guardians must have switched the X-ray or something. They'd saved him — and the mission.

Whatever Mr. Flute and Mr. Jinks had done, Tomm was glad.

No one knew he was an alien.

Chapter 11

THE HIGH COMMAND

"Um, when can I go back to the orphanage?" Tomm asked.

One of the doctors flipped through Tomm's chart. "Well, as we were just explaining," he said, "you are seriously injured. We'd like to keep you here overnight, at least."

"Out of the question," Mr. Flute said, shaking his head. "We'd like to bring Tomm back to the orphanage at once. Our staff nurses are the best in the state."

"I don't doubt it," one of the doctors said, "but Tomm is our patient, and we'd advise —"

Mr. Flute put up his hand to stop the doctor. "It's not your decision," he said. "We are the boy's guardians, and we will decide what care he gets."

Tomm sighed with relief.

"If you insist, then of course we will release him from our care," one doctor said.

"You'll have to sign some forms," the other doctor said. He shuffled through his folder and pulled out the papers.

Mr. Jinks stepped over and took the pen to sign the papers. While he did, Mr. Flute put a firm hand on Tomm's shoulder. "Don't worry," he said, grinning at the boy. "You'll be out of here in no time."

Chapter 12

THE SPY

Aug. 3

Soon, Tomm sat in the backseat of the dark, tinted-window station wagon. Beside him was Mr. Jinks.

Mr. Flute drove. He guided the long car slowly out of the hospital parking lot.

"You've had quite a day," Mr. Flute said. He looked at Tomm in the rearview mirror and smiled.

The black station wagon rolled down Main Street toward the center of Ravens Pass.

Tomm looked out the window at the Earthlings on the sidewalks. As always, they stopped to watch the mysterious car pass.

None of the Earthlings had any idea of what was coming from beyond the Solar System.

"But it all ended okay," Tomm said.

Mr. Jinks sneezed.

Mr. Flute laughed. "It certainly did," he said. "It ended quite well indeed. And now our mission can go on as planned."

Tomm blinked. "Hey!" he said. "Does that mean you've caught the spy?"

Mr. Jinks sighed.

Mr. Flute nodded happily. "We certainly did," he said.

Tomm sat back and relaxed. "I knew you two would take care of everything," he said.

Mr. Flute guided the car gently off Main Street, but rather than turning right toward the orphanage, he turned left.

"Are we going to the highway?" Tomm asked. He leaned forward.

Mr. Jinks put his hand on Tomm's shoulder and pulled him back.

"Please, sit back," Mr. Flute said. "Yes, we're going to the highway. You're to meet with the high command at once. They have a landing party in a field about an hour north of here."

"The high command?" Tomm said. He looked at Mr. Jinks, then at Mr. Flute in the rearview mirror. "Because of my accident? Am I badly injured?"

"Injured?" Mr. Flute said. He giggled. "Well, you saw the X-rays."

Tomm chuckled. "Oh, but those weren't my X-rays," he said. "You switched them, so the doctors wouldn't know who I really was."

Mr. Jinks coughed.

Mr. Flute grinned. "We did no such thing," he said.

Tomm's gut flipped.

"But if you didn't switch the X-rays," Tomm said, "that would mean I'm . . ."

"Exactly," Mr. Flute said. "An Earthling. You are the spy."

ABOUT THE AUTHOR

STEVE BREZENOFF is the author of dozens of chapter books for young readers and two novels for young adults. Some of his creepiest ideas show up in dreams, so most of the Ravens Pass stories were written in his pajamas. He lives in St. Paul, Minnesota, with his wife and their son.

ABOUT THE ILLUSTRATOR

TOM PERCIVAL was born and raised in the wilds of Shropshire, England, a place of such remarkable natural beauty that Tom decided to sit in his room every day, drawing pictures and writing stories. But that was all a long time ago, and much has changed since then. Now, Tom lives in Bristol, England, where he sits in his room all day, drawing pictures and writing stories while his patient girlfriend, Liz, and their son, Ethan, keep him company.

GLOSSARY

ALIEN (AY-lee-uhn)—a creature from another planet

COMMUNICATES (kuh-MYOO-nuh-kayts)—sends a message

EQUIPMENT (i-KWIP-muhnt)—tools and machines needed for a specific purpose

GEOLOGICAL (jee-uh-LAHJ-ik-uhl)—having to do with soil and rock

GUARDIAN (GARD-ee-uhn)—someone who is not the parent of a child, but who has the responsibility to look after him or her

IDENTITY (eye-DEN-ti-tee)—who a person is

MISSION (MISH-uhn)—a job or task

ORPHAN (OR-fuhn)—a child whose parents are dead

ORPHANAGE (OR-fuh-nij)—a place where orphans live

RESIDENTS (REZ-uh-duhnts)—people who live somewhere

SENSOR (SEN-sur)—an instrument that finds or checks something

UNCONSCIOUS (uhn-KON-shuhss)—not awake

DISCUSSION QUESTIONS

1. Do you believe in aliens? Explain your answer.

2. In this series, Ravens Pass is a town where crazy things happen. Has anything spooky or creepy ever happened in your town? Talk about stories you have heard.

3. When did you figure out that Tomm was an Earthling? What were the clues that told you?

WRITING PROMPTS

1. What happens next? Write a short story that extends this book.

2. Imagine that an alien comes to live in your town. Write a guidebook that helps the alien enjoy his or her stay.

3. Write a newspaper article describing the events in this book.

THE CROW'S

WEIRD EVENTS AT THE

Ravens Pass residents who have been paying attention for the past few years know that something's been weird at the Old Orphanage at the end of Main Street. No residents have ever been allowed in — even people who wanted to adopt a child. The men who ran the place, Jinx and Flute, didn't even try to fit in around town. And no one knows where the kids came from.

Strange stuff. So no one was surprised when the sheriff reported on Monday that there had been an emergency call from the orphanage. We've all been expecting something weird to happen there for a long time.

The weird thing was that when officers arrived, the building was empty. No furniture. No appliances. No orphans.

EYE

OLD ORPHANAGE

The sheriff told reporters that there was a thick layer of dust covering the place, as if no one had been there in years.

So what are residents of Ravens Pass supposed to think?

The sheriff gave one more detail. Apparently, there was a large circle burned into the grass in the backyard.

And that's all they found at the Old Orphanage.

Mr. Jinks and Mr. Flute

MORE DARK TALES

WITCH MAYOR

There's a story going around that the mayor of Ravens Pass is a witch. Could it be true?

CURSES FOR SALE

Weird things happen after Jace buys an old toy car at a garage sale. Is the toy cursed?

THE SLEEPER

The old orphanage on the outskirts of Ravens Pass? It's full of aliens ready to take over the planet.

NEW IN TOWN

When Andy is threatened, a new kid protects him. But there's something very strange about the new kid in town . . .

RAVENS PASS

LOOKING FOR ALL TYPES OF CREEPY CRAWLY SPOOKY GHOULISH TALES?

CHECK OUT
WWW.CAPSTONEKIDS.COM
FOR MORE FROM RAVENS PASS!

Find cool websites and more books like this one at www.facthound.com.

Just type in the Book ID: 9781434237927